WHISTLER'S HOLLOW

WHISTLER'S HOLLOW

BY

DEBBIE DADEY

BLOOMSBURY
CHILDREN'S
BOOKS

11-02

Library of Congress Cataloging-in-Publication Data
Dadey, Debbie. Whistler's Hollow / Debbie Dadey. p. cm. Summary: In 1920,
eleven-year-old Lillie Mae, recently orphaned, goes to live with her loving great-aunt
and great-uncle in their Kentucky farm house, where she learns the truth
about several secrets.
ISBN 1-58234-789-1 (alk. paper)
[1. Orphans—Fiction. 2. Great-uncles—Fiction. 3. Great-aunts—Fiction. 4.
Secrets—Fiction. 5. Kentucky—Fiction.] I. Title
PZ7.D128 Wh 2002   [Fic]—dc21   2001052578

First U.S. Edition 2002
Printed in Great Britain

1 3 5 7 9 10 8 6 4 2

Bloomsbury USA Children's Books
175 Fifth Avenue
New York, New York 10010

To my grandmother
Lillie Mae Bailey

1
THE END

Daddy had names for people like Aunt Helen, but he never said them around Mama. So it wasn't surprising when Aunt Helen got rid of me as fast as she could after Mama died. Aunt Helen took me to the train depot and rubbed a dirty spot off my cheek with her white gloves. People rushed around us on the platform, but I felt like I was in a foggy dream. I guess the fog was the black belching smoke of the coal-burning train, but maybe it was the shock of being sent all by myself across Kentucky on my very first train ride.

"Lillie Mae, you be a good girl when you get to your uncle Dallas," Aunt Helen told me with a sniff. "You're eleven years old and you can be a big help to him and Esther. You go on now."

"Yes, ma'am," I said, hesitating before I walked up the steep train steps. "If you hear from Daddy, please tell him where I am."

Aunt Helen pressed her lips together in a frown. "Lillie Mae, that is not going to happen. You need to get that through your head."

"But…" I begged. Aunt Helen said Daddy was killed in the war, but I didn't believe her. After all, my old friend Melissa K. Reynolds had gotten a telegram when her brother Fred was killed. We never got one, so I knew my daddy was alive. Peace had been declared over a year ago, so I knew Daddy would be back home soon and he'd be looking for me.

"Good-bye," Aunt Helen said, shoving me toward the steps.

Inside the train I felt the stiffness of the green velour seat through my cotton dress. People of all sizes and shapes sat around me. I bit my lip and wondered if Aunt Helen would tell Daddy where I was. I sat up straight and knew he'd find me, no matter what. Daddy could charm the socks off a dead man; that's what Mama had always said.

He could certainly get Aunt Helen to tell him where I was.

A big lady sat next to me with a blue hatbox and newspaper on her lap. She nodded to me and started reading the newspaper. It was dated September 30, 1920. *The Courier-Journal's* headlines blasted about hard times in baseball: "1920 Series Fixed."

I knew about hard times. My insides felt numb from everything that had happened this last week. Losing Mama didn't seem real. How could she be gone?

Things had changed so quickly. On Monday I had gone to school in the morning. By that afternoon Mama was dead, killed in an accident at the factory where she worked. Aunt Helen took everything out of our apartment, including me. Aunt Helen was Mama's sister, but that didn't keep Aunt Helen from selling nearly everything from our apartment. The things she couldn't sell she stuffed in a box in her attic. "I need the money to pay the funeral expenses," Aunt Helen had said. "I've never had a husband to pay my way, you know."

I nodded. Daddy had always said that no man could stand Aunt Helen for more than fifteen minutes at a time. I guess that's why Aunt Helen never thought too much of Daddy. And since I was partly my daddy, Aunt Helen didn't think too much of me either. After living at her house just one week, she put me on the nine o'clock westbound for Henderson, Kentucky.

Through the train window I saw Aunt Helen hand the conductor a cardboard suitcase tied together with a cord. Then the black smoke churned around her and she disappeared from sight. You'd think she would at least wave to her only niece, but she left without even a nod toward me. I wondered what had happened to Mama's tan leather suitcase. Either kept or sold by Aunt Helen like everything else, I figured. Because of her I didn't have anything to remind me of Mama, except the one thing I'd taken.

Daddy had given Mama a little glass bluebird the color of the sky. Mama kept it on her bedroom windowsill. I liked to look at it, although I had never touched it for fear of breaking it. Mama always said that a bluebird on your windowsill meant good luck. I guessed Aunt Helen believed it too. That morning before we'd left for the train station, I'd seen the bluebird on Aunt Helen's windowsill and without asking, I'd taken it and hidden it in my dress pocket. It felt cool and calming, a reminder of Mama.

The train headed toward relatives I'd never met before. It had taken Aunt Helen three days even to remember about them and another four days to find out if they were still alive. Uncle Dallas was my daddy's uncle, my great-uncle. Daddy had spent his teenage years helping on the farm after his parents had died. When he'd talked about it, Daddy had made the farm sound like a magical place, but he hadn't seen it for many years. We'd never had the money to travel across the state to visit.

The train lurched into the countryside with a loud blast of steam. I lay my forehead on the dusty window and stared for a long time. We rumbled past a family sitting on a grassy hill sharing a picnic lunch. A family—I knew I would never have that feeling of belonging again. My teacher, Mrs. Comer, had read us a book about a magic lamp and getting wishes. If I could have a wish, it would be to have my family back again, back in our own apartment with our own things.

I wondered what had happened to the Raggedy Ann doll Daddy had bought me before he'd left to fight in the war. I'd slept with it every single night since then. At least, I had until the week before, when Aunt Helen had taken everything away. Anger bubbled inside me. How I hated Aunt Helen. It seemed like she'd taken away my entire life. She'd be sorry when Daddy came home and found out what she'd done. Still, I wished I had my doll to hold and I wished Aunt Helen hadn't sent me away.

Late season flies buzzed around in the stuffy train. I even swatted at a curious bee. Behind me someone opened a package of bologna. It smelled so good, I wished I could have a bite. I hadn't had breakfast, and Aunt Helen hadn't given me anything to eat on the train. She'd said it would be better not to eat so I wouldn't have to go to the privy. "Don't go getting off the train until the conductor says you're in Henderson," she said. "If you get lost, there'll be no one to look for you."

When the train finally stopped in Henderson, I couldn't see anything outside the window—only darkness.

"Henderson, ahead of schedule!" the conductor

shouted. I hesitated. What if nobody was out there in the night to meet me? How would I know Uncle Dallas and Aunt Esther? I'd never even seen a picture of them. What if I went home with the wrong person? What if a murderer lurked in the shadows?

The burly conductor looked over his shoulder and yelled again, "Henderson!"

I gulped and walked down the aisle to the front of the train car. A little old lady with crooked teeth smiled at me. Her smile gave me enough courage to grab my cardboard suitcase. My other hand clung to the bluebird in my pocket. I walked down the train steps into the dark, cool night. The train pulled away, leaving me in a cloud of black smoke and very much alone.

2

UNCLE DALLAS

There was no one stirring near the train station in the town of Henderson. No one. Across from the station a pond glistened in the moonlight. Everything was so still, I could hear bullfrogs croaking on the banks.

After a few minutes I heard a loud noise and a big shiny black car drove by. Maybe Uncle Dallas was rich and I wouldn't have to worry about money for food or trying to pay bills like Mama had. The big black car slowed down. My heart pounded, but the car went on.

I sat on the wooden bench outside the closed depot with what my daddy called a stiff upper lip. I thought about going behind a bush to relieve myself, but the shadows looked like they would grab me up. A dog howled in the distance and crickets hummed all around. After about five minutes of sitting in the dark, my lips started trembling and tears welled in my eyes.

What if nobody came? Why had Aunt Helen sent me so far away? Couldn't I have stayed at her house and polished her mahogany furniture? After all, it was the house her parents—my grandparents—had left her. Surely they would have wanted me to live there too. I wouldn't have eaten that much. I could have cooked and cleaned for her. I'd done it a lot ever since Mama had started working at the factory. Mama. What would Mama think to see me out so late so far from home? She wouldn't even let me go down to the corner store after five o'clock for fear of ruffians. We'd stayed home at night. Mama would read or sew while I did my studies. Sometimes Mama was so tired from the factory, she'd fall asleep on the settee. I'd take away her book or sewing and put a quilt over her. Sometimes I'd snuggle beside her and we'd sleep together.

I held my glass bluebird tight when a big black crow landed on the depot sign, not more than five feet away from me. It stared at me with shining black eyes, and it looked as lonely as I felt. Somehow, with the bird there I didn't feel quite so alone. I wiped my tears. "I guess it's just you and me," I said, which was a funny thing to say to a bird. My mama used to say it to me all the time after Daddy went off to the war.

That was when a horse and wagon rumbled up. The tallest man I'd ever seen popped off the seat and leaped down beside me. He swept off his straw hat, revealing a patch of white hair. He bowed before me and asked, "Do I have the pleasure of meeting Miss Lillie Mae Worth?"

I had to giggle at the sight of this skinny, old man bowing down before me. His faded Blue Buckle overalls stretched at the shoulders as he bent down. He wore a clean blue shirt and his hands were rough, like a farmer's. That was fine with me. Daddy always said that farm work was honest work.

I curtsied as Aunt Helen had told me to and said, "Pleasure to meet you. I'm Lillie Mae."

"I'm your uncle Dallas, and I'm mighty pleased to meet you." He grabbed me in a bear hug and held me tight. He smelled freshly scrubbed of lye soap. Funny thing was, I didn't mind this strange man hugging me. It'd been a long while since I'd had a hug, and it felt right good.

He let me go and smiled, showing the lines of age on his face. He had a nice face though, and it reminded me of my daddy.

Uncle Dallas helped me into the wagon and put my box in the back.

"Now, I'm mighty sorry I wasn't here a bit earlier. Your aunt Esther wanted to come, but she's been feeling poorly. She'll have my hide when she finds out I was late."

"I didn't mind," I lied, settling onto the hard wooden wagon seat. "And we don't even have to tell Aunt Esther."

Uncle Dallas laughed and clicked to his old white horse, "Get home, Buster." Buster shook his mane and started off in the direction he'd come. We rolled past a few dark double-story buildings before entering a wooded area. The tall trees nearly cut out the moonlight.

"Esther thought you might be hungry, so she sent this," Uncle Dallas said, handing me a big piece of brown wrapping paper.

"Thank you," I said, tearing apart the wrapping to find a huge ham sandwich. I wolfed it down. The soft bread and sweet ham on my tongue tasted like the sandwiches Mama used to make for Saturday lunch with Daddy.

Uncle Dallas raised one eyebrow at my horrible manners and handed me a Mason jar filled with apple cider. "Didn't they feed you on that train?" he asked.

"No, sir," I said, trying to remember to mind my manners. And then, because I was afraid to wait any longer, I said softly, "They didn't have a privy either."

Uncle Dallas stopped the wagon beside a stand of trees. "Watch out for critters," he suggested.

I looked at the trees for a minute before I figured out that I was supposed to go there. I was so glad to go, I didn't even worry about snakes or skunks or such. Even so, I scrambled back into the wagon as quickly as I could. Uncle Dallas clicked Buster on our way. Uncle Dallas drove in peaceful silence. I was grateful he didn't talk. I didn't want to talk about Mama being dead. The buzz of the cicadas kept us company.

It seemed like we drove forever into the night before we turned down a dirt driveway and Uncle Dallas said, "Whoa" to Buster.

In the moonlight I saw the house. Every window was dark except one downstairs. A huge porch ran the whole length of the front and a swing creaked in the evening breeze.

A bird or a bat flew up past the attic window. The night sky overflowed with stars. I'd never seen so many at once. I looked around and it was completely dark everywhere. There were no neighbors close by that I could see. Always before I'd had neighbors within shouting distance. I felt so far away from everything, so tiny compared with the huge sky.

Inside, the house smelled old. Older than Aunt Helen's. Older than my school building. Older than the church Mama and I had gone to for as long as I could remember.

The kitchen didn't have much in it but a worn oak table and chairs, a huge wood-burning stove, a hutch, and a dry sink. The coal oil lantern cast an amber glow over the room.

"I told Aunt Esther not to wait up. You'll meet

her in the morning when she's rested," Uncle Dallas told me.

"It's a nice house," I said in a squeaky whisper.

Uncle Dallas smiled. "It's home. Your home now too."

I followed Uncle Dallas and the lantern up the tiny back staircase. The wooden stairs creaked, and darkness crept all around me. I felt like a tiny dot of light in a river of blackness. Uncle Dallas sat the lantern on a night table and pointed to a tall bed. "Good night," he whispered. "I'll take care of the lantern later."

"Good night and thank you," I whispered back. He left me the lantern and my cardboard suitcase before disappearing into the dark hall. I hurried into my nightgown and jumped under the heavy quilt before the shadows could get me. The feather bed swallowed me up. I was so tired, I fell fast asleep.

Sometime in the middle of the night I awoke with a start. It was blacker than Aunt Helen's cellar. Something had awakened me, but I didn't know what. I heard a shuffling sound and smelled something terrible. Not an old smell. It was a rotten food smell that turned my stomach. To me, it smelled like death. Did this happen to people before they died? Did they smell death? Did death come to get you like a horrible stinking hand in the dark?

3

AUNT ESTHER

I dove deeper under the covers, squeezing my eyes shut. My throat tightened, so I didn't think I could scream even if I tried. I pulled the pillow over my head to block out the sounds and smells, the sounds and smells of death.

I guess it worked because the next thing I knew morning came in through my window. Death had passed me by.

"Good morning, my Lillie Mae," a soft voice said.

"Mama!" I shouted, throwing off my covers and sitting bolt upright.

But it wasn't Mama. It was a tiny woman no bigger than my old friend Melissa K. Reynolds, who was taller than me but not by much. Sunlight from the window framed the woman's hair like a halo. "Sorry," she said quietly. "It's just your aunt Esther."

"Oh," I said, slumping down. I don't know what I'd been thinking. How could Mama be here? She was dead, after all. Still, for a moment Aunt Esther had sounded like Mama and it had been so sweet.

Aunt Esther moved slowly around the bed, picking my dress up off the floor, where I'd laid it last night, not knowing what else to do with it. It embarrassed me that I hadn't done the right thing. Aunt Esther patted the bureau and put my dress on top. "After breakfast you can put your things in here," she said.

Remembering that I was a guest, I hopped out of bed and curtsied. "Thank you. It's very nice to meet you."

Aunt Esther raised an eyebrow and smiled. "You're quite welcome, but remember, you're family, so there's no need to stand on ceremony at Whistler's Hollow."

"Whistler's Hollow?" I asked.

Aunt Esther nodded. "That's the nickname this farm has had for as long as I can recall."

"It's a nice name," I said politely, thinking it was the strangest name I'd ever heard. I wondered what kind of people would name a farm something so funny.

"Come down for breakfast as soon as you're dressed," Aunt Esther told me.

Aunt Esther stood at the stove turning flapjacks as I came down the steps. Uncle Dallas poured coffee from a blue metal pot into three cups on the table. Steam whirled toward his white head. I noticed the yellow-and-white checked kitchen curtains and the way the sun filled the warm room with a lemony glow.

Aunt Esther smiled at me and wiped her hands on her apron—something I knew Aunt Helen would not have liked. All my life Aunt Helen had told me what a lady should and shouldn't do. But Aunt Helen had never put her arms around me and hugged me like Aunt Esther did just then. "I hope you're hungry," she said. "We have flapjacks, sausage, eggs, biscuits, blackberry jelly, and coffee."

"Esther thinks I brought home an army last night to feed, instead of one beautiful young lady,"

Uncle Dallas teased.

"There's nothing wrong with having a good breakfast," Aunt Esther said, leaning her hand onto the table for support.

Uncle Dallas guided her into a chair. "You take it easy now, Esther. I'll get the grub." He whistled and flipped the flapjacks into the air.

"This one is yours, Lillie Mae," Uncle Dallas said. "Lift your plate up."

I'd been taught to mind, so I held my plate up. Uncle Dallas tossed the flapjack my way.

"Dallas Worth!" Aunt Esther shrieked. "Have you lost your mind?"

Uncle Dallas laughed when I caught the flapjack as if I did it every day. "I've never missed a plate yet," Uncle Dallas crooned.

Aunt Esther bent her head down, trying to hide a smile. "Lillie Mae's going to think she's landed in the home for crazy old people."

"She has," Uncle Dallas said seriously, before heaping more flapjacks onto my plate. I ate until I figured one more bite and my buttons would pop through the air like Uncle Dallas's flapjacks.

"That's it," Aunt Esther said after we'd all eaten

our fill. She pointed to Uncle Dallas. "It's time for all the crazy old men to leave the kitchen."

Uncle Dallas shook his head. "I'll clean up. I don't want you to work too hard."

Aunt Esther waved him away like a queen to a royal servant. "Be gone, crazy man. Lillie Mae will help me."

I started clearing the plates to the sink. Before Uncle Dallas left, he lifted a big pot of water from the stove and poured it into a dishpan.

"Know any good songs?" Aunt Esther asked.

"Ma'am?"

"Do you know any songs to sing?" she asked again, chipping soap into the big dish of hot water.

I shrugged and looked down at my hands. Mama and Daddy had sung lots of songs before the war, but it seemed like so long ago. Aunt Esther touched my shoulder with a gentle hand. "I'm sorry," she said. "I guess you haven't had a lot to sing about lately."

I shrugged again, not knowing exactly how to answer. "I knew your papa," Aunt Esther said, "but I never got to Louisville to meet your mama. Would you mind letting me see a picture?"

"I... I wouldn't mind," I told her truthfully, "but I don't have one."

"That's too bad. I guess your mama never got around to having her picture made."

"No, she did. My aunt Helen has several of them. She has all my mama's things," I explained.

"You mean you didn't get any of your mama's belongings?" Aunt Esther asked.

I gulped and shook my head. I wasn't about to say anything about the bluebird I'd hidden behind the starched curtains in my bedroom. I didn't want to have to give it back to Aunt Helen. I busied myself putting the dishes into the dishpan, trying not to let Aunt Esther see my guilty face.

Aunt Helen was Mama's only sister. I figured that Mama's things rightfully went to her, but I sure would have liked to have had at least one picture of Mama and Daddy. I remembered the one of them that had sat on a table beside my baby picture. The wooden frame was painted to look like gold. Mama's hair was done up in a twist and she had on a silky dress that she'd borrowed from a lady in our apartment building. Daddy looked spiffy in his tan doughboy uniform with the brass buttons. That picture was taken at the going-away party Melissa K. Reynolds's parents had given before Daddy left for the war. I think the Reynolds had hoped that sending my daddy off in style might bring their own son good luck, but that was before the Reynolds had gotten their telegram.

Aunt Esther's mouth set in a straight line that I took to mean trouble.

"I think I need to write me a letter," she said. "Get me a sharp pencil and paper from that drawer."

Aunt Esther sat for quite a while writing a letter while I finished the dishes. She didn't tell me what it said, but I hoped she was telling Aunt Helen how helpful I was with washing the dishes.

After I'd wiped everything that could be wiped, I went upstairs and put my three extra sets of panties and socks into the bureau. I went ahead and put my other dress in the second drawer, even though the dress was too small. Maybe I could make an apron out of the skirt someday. I remembered when Mama had sewed the dress. It'd been winter and I'd made soup to keep us warm. Mama had sewed all afternoon as the soup had simmered.

Papa had been out somewhere.

I put my sweater on against the chill before walking down the steps into the kitchen. Aunt Esther was resting her head on the table, so instead of disturbing her I went out into the backyard.

I walked around a chicken coop, an outhouse, and a barn. They looked a lot like Old Man Henessy's back home. Old Man Henessy was a farmer friend of Daddy's. In the front of Uncle Dallas's house there were half a dozen rosebushes with blooms still withering and leaves scattered around the yard. I figured this would be a good time for me to earn my keep. I found a rake in the barn and started gathering up all the leaves. Soon I had a big pile, but didn't know what to do with them. It would be a shame for a puff of wind to ruin all my hard work. I was thinking about it when a voice came from the road.

"Ghosts live there, you know."

I jumped a mile. I turned around and looked at a boy about my age, every bit as skinny as me only quite a bit taller. "Hello," I said.

He pointed to the attic and repeated, "Ghosts live there, you know."

I gulped and stared at the dark attic window. I didn't know what to say to the boy, but it didn't matter. He turned to leave, calling over his shoulder, "You're crazy to live in that old haunted house."

⚘ 4 ⚘
SCHOOL

"Let's go," Uncle Dallas said from behind me.

"Go where?" I asked, wondering if Uncle Dallas had heard the strange boy.

Uncle Dallas slapped his straw hat on his white head. "Why, to school, of course. Isn't that what girls your age do?"

"Sure," I said. I loved school at home. There I read wonderful books, saw my friends, and listened to Mrs. Comer's stories. I wanted my new school to be like that.

Uncle Dallas and I bumped along in the wagon down the dusty road. We passed farmhouses that I hadn't even seen in the dark last night. Uncle Dallas had his violin case on the wagon bed, and he whistled. It seemed strange for him to be carrying a case to school, but I didn't dwell on it. My mind worried about my new school. Would the girls like me? Would the boys be nice? Would I be smart enough?

Uncle Dallas stopped whistling and pointed straight ahead. "There she is—Paggett School."

My old school had been two stories high and made of brick. A small wooden building made up Paggett School. Girls and boys ran around outside, kicking a ball. None of them looked at me. "Don't worry," Uncle Dallas said. "You'll be fine."

"Aren't you coming in?" I asked, not wanting him to leave.

Uncle Dallas shook his head and grinned. "I haven't been to school yet and I don't plan on starting today. You go on now."

I gulped. Uncle Dallas must have felt my fear because he gave me a hug and a little pat on the back. "See you for lunch. You just walk down this road to home."

I walked straight through all those boys and girls, and up a small set of steps. Inside there was only one room. A man looked up over his reading glasses at me. "Yes?" he said impatiently.

"I, I'm Lillie Mae Worth.... I'm a new student," I whispered.

The man slapped his pencil down on the desk. "Haven't I got enough already?"

I didn't know what to say, but I don't think the teacher would have listened anyway. He pointed to a desk at the back of the room. As soon as I took my seat, he rang a big hand-bell on his desk. Boys and girls of all sizes and ages appeared through the door. They stared at me like I was a rat in a church pew. The new teacher didn't waste any time.

"Open your readers to page nineteen," he said. I didn't have a reader, so I just sat there while the other students read silently. I wanted to ask the teacher for one, but I was too scared. He didn't seem like the helping kind. No one offered to share any books the entire morning, and the teacher never bothered to give me one.

By the time I walked home for lunch, I was ready to cry. Not one boy or girl had even talked to me. I might as well have been the dust on the bookshelves.

"Welcome home," Aunt Esther said with asmile

as I came in the kitchen door at noon. I'm embarrassed to say that I started bawling right then and there.

"Oh, honey, what's wrong?" Aunt Esther asked, gathering me up in her arms.

I couldn't say anything, I just cried. Aunt Esther sat me on her lap and smoothed my hair. "It's all right," she whispered. "You go ahead and cry. You've had too much to deal with lately. First, your papa dying and now your mama...."

I jumped off her lap and yelled, "My daddy isn't dead!"

"But..." Aunt Esther said softly.

"He isn't dead!" I shouted. Then, because I didn't know what else to do, I ran out the door.

I walked back to the school feeling a hundred years old. I felt miserable for talking to Aunt Esther that way. After all, she'd been nothing but kind to me. But I couldn't let her say that Daddy was dead. He wasn't. He couldn't be. I took a deep breath and blew it out long and slow. That helped a little, although my belly grumbled from hunger. If I'd been smart, I'd have grabbed some of the lunch that Aunt Esther had made for me.

SCHOOL

The school yard was deserted. Only one girl sat under a tree, eating from a lunch bucket. I went around to the side of the school and sat alone in the dust.

I thought about Mama and Daddy and how long it'd been since we'd all been together. Even before Daddy had left for the war, he'd been too busy to do things. He'd always had something he'd had to do. But there had been a time when we'd gone on picnics, walked to the movies and dances together. All that was before the war, of course. The war had ruined everything.

When I walked up the steps after the lunch bell sounded, someone talked to me. I wished they hadn't. "Hey, crazy girl!" a kid yelled.

I whirled around to look into the blue eyes of the skinny boy I'd seen at Whistler's Hollow that morning. I tried to be nice. "Hello," I said, raising my hand in greeting. "I'm Lillie Mae Worth. I'm new."

"You don't look new. And you couldn't get me to stay at Whistler's Hollow for a dollar. Don't you know it's haunted?" A crowd of kids gathered around and stared at me.

"Why do you keep saying that?" I asked, my face

turning red.

The boy shrugged. "That's what everybody says. Hey, maybe you don't mind because you are a ghost."

"You take that back!" I shouted. "That's a lie."

A blonde girl spoke up. "Paul, why don't you leave her alone?"

Paul ignored the girl. "Maybe Lillie Mae's just a ghost in faded old clothes. Don't dead people get new clothes every hundred years or so?"

"Why are you saying such lies?" I asked him. "Take it back."

Paul pushed me in the shoulder. "Ghost," he said.

I don't know why, but for some reason I pushed him back. I'd never fought before. Maybe it was everything that was happening to me lately, but I couldn't stand him talking to me like that in front of everyone. When he pushed again, I pushed back and soon we were in a full-fledged scuffle.

Our teacher made us stop. He glared at us from the top of the stairs. "Inside right now!"

"Now you've done it," Paul complained.

And that is how I got a spanking on my first day

of school in Henderson, Kentucky. Paul got one too and, judging from the look Paul gave me afterward, things weren't going to get any better at Paggett School.

By the time I walked back to Whistler's Hollow, I felt as if my heart had been stomped to bits. I kicked at a rock in the road and longed for home— for my old school and friends. Melissa K. Reynolds had probably found someone else to walk to school with by now. I'd never have any friends here.

The only thing besides my pride (and my bottom) that had suffered from my scrapping with Paul was my dress. There was a good-sized rip in the sleeve. It wouldn't take much mending to fix it. I could do it easy if I could find some thread. Mama had taught me to sew when I was six. My dress was already faded, but now it was ripped and stained from rolling in the dirt with Paul. I hoped I could fix the rip and wash out the dirt stains before anyone at Whistler's Hollow saw them. What would Uncle Dallas and Aunt Esther think of me?

Of course, my bottom hurt a lot. The teacher must have given lots of spankings, because he was quite good at it. I figured I'd have trouble sitting for days. I just hoped that Paul got whipped harder than me.

"Ow!" Something hit me in the shoulder.

"Ow!" A rock smacked me in the leg. Paul was throwing rocks at me. One whizzed by my ear. I didn't stop to yell. I ran.

I ran until I thought my lungs would burst. I stopped and panted. Paul hadn't followed. At least, I didn't think so. I picked up five good throwing stones just in case.

Why was he doing this to me?

❦ 5 ❦
MENDING

When I finally trudged into Whistler's Hollow, the house was empty. The only sound was the mantel clock in the parlor. Tick. Tick. Tick. "Hello?" I said faintly, more than a little relieved that no one could see my torn, dirty dress.

I found a needle and thread in a sewing basket. In my room I fixed my ripped sleeve as best I could. My only other dress was tight, but at least it was clean. I washed my newly mended dress in the dishpan in the kitchen before laying it out to dry on a bush behind the barn. I hoped it would dry before anyone noticed it. I didn't want to lie about what had happened, but I didn't want to talk about it either.

After that I didn't know what to do with myself. I wished I had a good book to read. Maybe Aunt Esther had some—maybe she even had a school-book I could use. I walked around the wallpapered parlor checking for books, and stopped at the fireplace. Several old photos and tintypes sat in wood frames on the mantel. One looked like Aunt Esther and Uncle Dallas on their wedding day. Some pictures were of people I'd never seen before. I wondered if I was related to any of them. I picked up one dusty frame that showed a young boy and his parents. My grandparents had died before I was born, but I knew that young boy. It was my father.

I'll bet I stared at that picture for half an hour. Tears welled up in my eyes and things got blurry. "Oh, Daddy," I whispered, "please come home. I need you. You're all I have now." Daddy had been gone for so long, sometimes it was hard to remember things about him. The picture brought it all back. I touched the photograph where a cowlick made his hair stick up on one side. His smile was still the same, at least the same as the last time I'd seen him.

He'd leaned out the window of the train and

waved along with hundreds of other soldiers. Mama
and I had waved back until his train had left the
station. That's when Mama had grabbed my hand.
She had tears running down her cheeks. It'd been
the first time she'd said, "I guess it's just you and
me." But it wasn't the last time. Now I guessed it
would be Daddy saying that, whenever he got
home. I didn't know what was taking him so long.
After all, the war had been over for a year. Mama
never would tell me when he was coming home.
Maybe he was wounded in a hospital somewhere,
getting better and missing me like I was missing
him. Maybe he was on a special secret mission
that put him in great danger. I didn't like to think
about what was wrong, so I hugged his picture to
my chest.

After that I got busy and dusted the photo-
graphs with a rag I found in the kitchen. I was trying to whistle softly when Aunt Esther came in the
room. I didn't realize she was there until she tapped
me on the shoulder. "Oh," I cried. "You startled me."

"Lillie Mae, I'm sorry I wasn't here when you
came in from school," Aunt Esther said. "I was
taking a nap."

It seemed strange for a grown woman to be taking a nap in the middle of the day, unless she was sick. "Are you ill?" I asked.

Aunt Esther smiled. "Just old," she said. "It's awful when your bones are older than your spirit."

I wiped my father's picture frame one more time and Aunt Esther clapped her hands. "Why, I'd plumb forgotten that I had that picture of Bobby. Why don't you keep that?"

"Do you mean it?" I asked.

Aunt Esther nodded. "Of course. You should have a picture of your daddy."

I lowered my eyes, remembering how mean I'd been to her at lunchtime. "I'm so sorry for the way I talked before," I said softly.

"Don't worry," she said. "A little shouting is good for the soul. Now run along and put that in your room."

"Thank you." I held the picture to my chest and headed toward the steps.

"Wait just a minute, young lady," Aunt Esther stopped me. "Let me see that dress."

I gulped. Aunt Esther had figured out what had happened. She knew I'd been in a fight and ripped my dress. What would she do to me?

"This dress looks awful small for you, honey," Aunt Esther said, turning up my skirt to check the hem. I knew for a fact that Mama had let the hem out twice.

"Do you have another one?" Aunt Esther asked, and I nodded.

"That one you had on this morning?" she asked, and I nodded again.

Aunt Esther tapped her chin. "Mmmm, we ought to be able to help you out."

"How are the lovely Worth ladies this afternoon?" Uncle Dallas said as he came into the room. He mopped his brow with a big kerchief and sat down in the wooden rocker.

"We were just talking about getting Lillie Mae some new clothes," Aunt Esther said. "I know! We'll go up in the attic. There's a trunk up there with lots of my old dresses. I bet there's one in there we can fix over for you."

Uncle Dallas stood up. "No need for you to go into the attic," he said. "I'll bring the trunk down and you two can go through it together."

Aunt Esther clapped her hands. "Thank you,

Dallas. This will be so much fun!"

True to his word, a few minutes later Uncle Dallas set the dusty trunk in the parlor and left us to it. Aunt Esther started digging through the trunk right away. "I saved these for my daughter," she said.

This seemed like a good time to ask what I'd been wondering. "Do you have children?"

"No, I'm sorry to say we never had any of our own," Aunt Esther said softly. "It's not that we didn't want any, mind you. I would have loved a whole houseful of noisy young'uns. It just never happened. But I'm glad I saved these. I think some might just fit you."

"It's sure nice of you," I told her.

"Look at this one, Lillie Mae. Isn't it a honey?" Aunt Esther pulled out of the trunk the most beautiful dress I'd ever seen. The white, shimmery material glowed when it moved. "I wore this when I was not much older than you. It was for a cotillion."

"A cotillion?" I asked.

"That's just the name for a fancy party for young girls," Aunt Esther explained. "My parents had a lot of money in those days. Our house at White Oaks was decorated with magnolia blossoms, and our cooks prepared enough food to feed an army. It was quite an affair." Aunt Esther had a faraway look on her face.

"It's a very pretty dress," I told her truthfully. "I've never seen one nicer."

Aunt Esther smiled and handed me the dress. "I can't believe it's in such good shape. I guess the mothballs helped. Try it on. We can wash the smell out later."

The dress did have a mothball smell, but another smell too. It was the rotten smell I'd smelled last night. I gulped, slipped out of my tight faded dress, and shyly stood in front of Aunt Esther with my petticoat. Aunt Esther didn't even seem to notice how old and stained it was, she just eased the cool fabric of the dress over my head, buttoned me up, and spun me around. "You look like an angel."

I felt like an angel too. I wished Mama or Daddy could have seen me. I hung my head down, but Aunt Esther didn't give me time to feel sad. "Lookie here," she said, pulling out a pair of white slippers that were sparkled with gold. "It's hard to believe my feet used to be so small. Try these on too."

They didn't fit. Aunt Esther had me pull off my heavy blue socks and then the shoes glided right on my bare feet as if they'd been made for me. Aunt Esther sat down on the settee and looked me over. "I don't think that's a proper school dress though. Let's see what else we can find. We can save that one for Christmas."

Christmas! I stared at the dress in the looking glass. I wouldn't still be here at Christmas. Daddy wouldn't let me be alone for Christmas. I knew he'd be here before then. Maybe Aunt Esther would give me the dress to take with me.

We found two dresses that were a bit too big that would work fine for school. "I'll take these in tonight and you'll be all set for tomorrow," Aunt Esther said.

"Thank you," I said softly, picking up Daddy's picture and holding it to my chest. Aunt Esther was being awfully kind. I felt guilty, but all I wanted was for Daddy to come so I could go home. The last thing I wanted was to go to school tomorrow. I knew Paul would be waiting for me.

❧ 6 ❧
SCHOOL

I had loved recess at my old school. Melissa K. Reynolds and I had jumped rope, sung songs, and talked. But recess at my new school was something different. I stood against the side of the building in the shadows and watched. I watched a group of girls jumping rope. I watched another group laughing, talking, and even singing. I watched a huge group of boys playing kick ball. Paul was one of them. Once he kicked the ball right beside my head. Slam! It hit with so much force, I was sure our teacher would come running. Paul laughed and raced away with the ball.

I stood and watched for a long time. Finally I got up my courage and walked over to a group of girls.

"Hello, I'm Lillie Mae. Can I play?" I asked.

A large girl with black hair looked me up and down. I knew her name to be Judy. I was grateful I had on my newly made-over dress. "We," Judy said, nodding to the girls around her, "don't like people who get Paul in trouble."

"But, I didn't…" I started to argue. Judy didn't give me a chance. She turned her back to me and laughed with her group. I walked back over to the wall, but after that I didn't talk to the other groups.

I didn't go home for lunch either. I didn't want Paul to knock me in the head with a rock. Aunt Esther had given me some cold biscuits and an apple in an old lunch pail. After everyone had left, there was one girl still sitting under a big tree. She was Alberta, a girl who never spoke much in class unless Mr. Price, our teacher, called on her. I thought about sitting beside her, but I still smarted from the way Judy had talked to me. I went around the corner of the building to hide from Paul, and sat in the dirt. The dry biscuits stuck in my throat and I felt as sorry for myself as I possibly could.

A big black bird landed not too far away. "I

remember you from the train station," I said. Then I looked around to make sure no one heard me talking to the bird. They'd probably put me in a hospital.

The bird looked at me and I looked at the bird. It was shiny black, almost blue. It didn't seem one bit scared of me. "How about some biscuit crumbs?" I whispered, tossing some toward the bird.

The bird picked at the crumbs. It stared at me a minute before flying away. "Don't go," I called. I didn't want to be alone.

Every day for the next few weeks I sat in the same spot for lunch and every day the crow came back. I was so grateful not to be alone that I shared my biscuits with it. One day the bird ate right out of my hand. I wished I could hold it, but some things you can't hold on to. So I just watched it eat out of my hand.

"Lordy, look at that bird," a girl whispered from the corner of the building. It was Alberta.

I jumped when Alberta spoke, and the bird flew away. "No, don't go," I called, but it was too late. The bird was gone. I had the sinking feeling that it wouldn't be back.

I glared at Alberta. "Why did you have to scare her away?" I yelled.

"Her?" she whispered. I just glared. I don't know why I thought the bird was a she. Somehow I just knew she was a girl. I also knew I was mad at Alberta for scaring the bird.

Alberta looked close to tears. "I'm sorry," she whispered before ducking back around the corner.

"No, wait," I said. Now I felt bad for hurting Alberta's feelings. Here she was the only one at school who'd bothered to try to be nice to me and I'd hollered at her. I slapped the dust off the back of my dress, collected my lunch pail, and followed her.

Alberta sat under the tree with her thin back to me. She was putting a napkin back into her lunch pail. "I shouldn't have yelled at you," I said softly.

Alberta didn't answer, so I tried again. "Why do you eat lunch here every day?" I asked, sitting beside her on the grass.

She looked at me with eyes so gray, they looked like smoke. Her straw-blonde hair and freckles didn't seem to match her serious eyes. "I live too far out to go home for lunch," she said softly. "What about you?"

I shrugged and told the truth. "I'm afraid Paul will throw rocks at me again." I knew I sounded like a big baby. I lowered my head, ashamed.

"Why does Paul hate you so much?" she asked.

I shook my head, glad to be able to talk to someone about it. I hadn't wanted to upset Aunt Esther, and I was embarrassed to tell Uncle Dallas. "I don't know, but he seems nice to everyone else."

"He is," Alberta said, glancing down at her rough hands, "except that he warned everyone to stay away from you or…"

"Or what?" I asked.

"Or they'd be sorry," she whispered. Together we both looked down the road to make sure no one saw us together. No one was coming.

"I don't want to get you in trouble," I told her.

Alberta smiled, showing two crooked front teeth. "We could talk and play while everyone is gone. Paul wouldn't find out."

I smiled back, so grateful that the bird had brought me and Alberta together.

❧ 7 ❧
MUSIC

"Play my favorite. It's been way too long," Aunt Esther told Uncle Dallas that evening. Uncle Dallas had killed a chicken and we'd fried it up in honor of my being with them a month. That meant it was a little over four weeks since Mama had died. Now we sat in the parlor, in what Aunt Esther called the "good room."

Uncle Dallas gave me a wink and put a polished fiddle under his chin. It was the first time I'd heard him play, although I'd seen him carrying the case every day. He filled the parlor with a sound like nothing I'd ever heard before. The sweetness rang in the air like angels in heaven. I stared at Uncle Dallas as he played the hymn "Amazing Grace."

The organist at my old church had sounded nothing like that.

"Sing it with me, Esther," Uncle Dallas said. Together they sang. I'd like to say it was beautiful, but it wasn't. Uncle Dallas's voice was shaky, but not bad to listen to. It was Aunt Esther's voice that sounded like a rusty tin can rattling around on the side of a gravel road. I'd never heard anyone sing so poorly.

"Come on, honey," Aunt Esther said. "Sing with us. You can't be any worse than me."

I knew that to be true, so I joined in. "'Through many dangers, toils, and snares I have already come.'" I winced a bit when Aunt Esther tried for the high note. "''Tis grace hath brought me safe thus far and grace will lead me home.'"

I sang the rest of the song, wanting to cover my ears. When we finished, Aunt Esther looked at me and said, "Why don't you pick one?"

"How about 'Old Dan Tucker'?" I asked, remembering the song that Daddy always whistled.

Aunt Esther grabbed my hands and pulled. "Lillie Mae, let's dance! Play for us, Dallas."

Uncle Dallas hesitated with his bow above the

strings. "Maybe you shouldn't dance, Esther. You need to take it easy."

"Pshaw. I'm feeling fine. Play, old man." Uncle Dallas did play and Aunt Esther spun me around. We all sang, " 'Get out of the way, Old Dan Tucker. You're too late to get your supper.' " We sang and danced and danced and sang. After we'd exhausted every verse we knew, Uncle Dallas whistled a verse for us. It sounded just like Daddy. I stopped dancing and sat down.

"Whew!" Aunt Esther said. "I'd better rest too." She fanned herself with a paper fan from Rudy-Rowland's Funeral Home. We listened as Uncle Dallas played and whistled.

Aunt Esther smiled. "My Dallas is a fine whistler. All the Worth men are. I guess they didn't name this place Whistler's Hollow for nothing."

When the music stopped, I worked up the nerve to ask Uncle Dallas, "Could you teach me that?"

"What?" he asked, taking a hankie from his overall pocket and wiping his mouth. "Whistling or fiddling?"

"Both," I said, even though I'd meant to say only whistling.

"I'd be prouder than a cat with a dead mouse," Uncle Dallas said. "Come here."

"You mean you'd teach me right now?" I'd asked Papa to teach me to whistle, but he'd always been too busy.

"Surely," Uncle Dallas said. "You know what they say. There's no time like the present."

Aunt Esther fanned while Uncle Dallas helped me hold the fiddle under my chin. It felt awkward and I wanted to tell him to forget about teaching me. Then he showed me how to run the bow over the strings to make them sing. After a few minutes he showed me how to play part of "Listen to the Mockingbird," one of Mama's favorites.

"You're a natural." Uncle Dallas beamed. "Now let's try the whistling."

I did try, but I didn't get much more out than a slow wind blowing through the tree limbs. Even Aunt Esther tried to show me how to hold my mouth. She let out a whistle that might have raised the dead. Mine was downright pitiful.

"Don't worry," Aunt Esther said, patting my hand. "It'll come. Time has a way of working every-thing out." She gave me a hug, and I had a feeling she wasn't really talking about whistling.

"Dallas, can you help this old woman up the stairs?" she asked. "I'm plumb worn out." Uncle Dallas laid his violin down and stooped to put his arm around Aunt Esther.

He helped her from the settee and up the steps. "Good night, Lillie Mae," Aunt Esther called. In a softer voice I heard her talk to Uncle Dallas. "I know I overdid it tonight, but it was such fun."

"It's all right," Uncle Dallas said gently. "You're almost well now."

I looked around the small room. Lace curtains hung from the two windows and crocheted doilies lay on the back of the settee and the stuffed chair. I touched the violin and felt a thrill. Maybe Uncle Dallas would keep teaching me. Wouldn't Mama and Daddy be proud then? I pulled my hand away when I remembered that Mama was dead. For a minute I felt like smashing the violin against the wall. What was the use? Why learn to play if Mama couldn't hear me?

Daddy. He'd be proud. Listening to the music would help ease the pain of losing Mama. I made up my mind that by the time Daddy got home, I'd be playing "Old Dan Tucker" just like Uncle Dallas. I could picture Daddy whistling while I played. I'd have to get to work right away, because he could get here at any time.

The parlor clock clicked away the minutes and I figured I'd better get to bed as well. I fell asleep with a smile, looking forward to playing the violin again.

Along about the middle of the night, something woke me. I felt cold to the bone when I heard the shuffling sound and smelled the horrible odor.

"Ghosts live there," Paul had said. Was he right? Was that what was making the noise? I lay still as glass for a few minutes, afraid even to breathe. Then I heard the shuffling sound again and a crash. I hopped out of bed. Maybe Aunt Esther needed help. Had she fallen? She had looked awfully tired when she'd gone to bed.

The wooden floor shot darts of cold through my bare feet as I inched along the hallway. The only light came from a moonlit hall window. I froze when I heard the shuffling again, but it didn't come from Aunt Esther and Uncle Dallas's bedroom. The noise came from behind a closed door.

I gulped and reached out to grab the doorknob.

"Lillie Mae!" Uncle Dallas shouted. "What are you doing out of bed?" I whirled around to see Uncle Dallas fully dressed and carrying a big sack.

"I... heard a noise from there," I said, pointing to the door.

Uncle Dallas shook his head. "That's to the attic. The noise is some loose shingles on the roof."

"But I smelled something terrible. Maybe it needs cleaning. If you'd like, I'll scrub it down tomorrow."

"NO!" Uncle Dallas shouted and came closer. "You are never to go up there."

I backed against the wall, away from Uncle Dallas. He came closer to me and grabbed my shoulder with one hand. "You are never to go in the attic, Lillie Mae! Do you understand?"

My mind flashed to Melissa K. Reynolds's drunken father hitting her with a switch. Would it be that way for me too? I nodded to Uncle Dallas and ran back into my bedroom. Under the quilts I cried myself to sleep.

❧ 8 ❧
PAUL

There were no flipping flapjacks the next morning. Only a bowl of warm oatmeal left on the table. After I ate the oatmeal, I cleaned up the dishes and swept the kitchen floor. I wandered outside and ended up sniffing the faded roses. I looked up at the roof to see if I could see the loose shingles Uncle Dallas had mentioned. As far as I could see, they were all nailed down tight.

The front screen door flew open and I flinched. Uncle Dallas stood on the front porch, his white hair waving wildly around his head. His eyes were red and he looked upset. "Lillie Mae, ride into town. Get the doctor, quick. Esther has taken a turn for the worse."

I didn't ask questions. I ran to the barn and grabbed Buster. At least I knew how to ride bareback from the time Mrs. Comer had brought her bay to school. I raced off in the direction of town. Aunt Esther had been so full of life last night when we'd danced. How could she be sick? Unless that was the reason, maybe she shouldn't have danced. If I hadn't been there, she wouldn't have danced. Maybe I was the reason she'd taken a turn for the worse. I tried to get Buster to go faster. By the time I neared the first house, I realized I didn't know where the doctor lived.

I hesitated for a second at the gate. What if one of the mean girls from school lived here? I had no choice but to jump off Buster and ask for help. The house needed painting worse than Whistler's Hollow, but the yard was trimmed and neat. The porch creaked when I stepped across it. Holding my breath I rapped on the door.

After a few minutes a lady about my mama's age opened the door. She was dressed in black and very pale, but smiled when she saw me. "Welcome," she said. "You must be Lillie Mae."

She surprised me by knowing my name. "Yes,

ma'am," I said.

The lady pointed back down toward Whistler's Hollow. "My son Paul works in the mornings for a farmer down the road a piece, before he goes to school. Paul and I think a lot of Esther and Dallas."

Paul! I couldn't believe my closest neighbor was Paul. I nodded, realizing we were wasting precious time. "It's nice to meet you, Mrs. Garrett. Could you tell me where the doctor lives? Uncle Dallas said for me to fetch him quick."

Mrs. Garrett's smile faded. She was all business. "Go to the first brick house you see. That's the doctor's."

I nodded my thanks and rushed out to the dirt road. A big black car slowed down as it passed me. I didn't pay it any mind, I just pulled myself back up on Buster. My chest was heaving along with Buster's by the time I saw a brick house. I pounded on the door.

There was no answer. What if the doctor was gone? What was I supposed to do? I pounded again.

The door creaked open. A little girl, no more than four, stared up at me, sucking her thumb. "Whatcha want?" she asked.

"I'm looking for the doctor," I explained.

"That's my daddy," she said proudly.

"Is he here? I need him now! My aunt's really sick."

"Come on," she said, turning and walking away. I followed her through the huge house to a back room, wishing she would hurry. "My name is Lucy," she told me before she tapped on the door.

"That's nice. My name is Lillie Mae."

The door swung open and a bearded man with rolled-up sleeves looked out. "Papa, this is Lillie Mae. Her aunt's dying."

My face burned. "I didn't say she was dying. Aunt Esther has taken a turn for the worse."

"I'll get my bag," the doctor said. In five minutes we were in the doctor's Model T, bouncing over the dirt road with Buster tied to the bumper.

"What's wrong with Esther?" the doctor asked.

"I don't know," I said. "She was fine last night when she was dancing."

"Dancing!" the doctor exploded. "I told her to take it easy."

I nodded. "So did Uncle Dallas."

"I'm glad somebody has some sense at

Whistler's Hollow." The doctor took his eyes from the road for a minute and introduced himself. "Folks around here call me Doc White. I hope you'll like living in Henderson."

"Thank you," I said politely.

I grabbed the side of the Model T as it jerked to a stop in front of Whistler's Hollow. Uncle Dallas yelled out the upstairs window, "Doc, get in here quick!"

9
VIOLIN

I was trying to whistle softly when Uncle Dallas came in the kitchen. I didn't realize he was there until he tapped me on the shoulder. "Oh," I cried. "Is Aunt Esther all right?"

Uncle Dallas put a finger to his lips. "Esther is sleeping," he said gently. "The doctor told her to stay in bed for at least a week."

I nodded. "Can I do something to help?"

Uncle Dallas reached out and gave me a big hug. "I'm sorry I snapped at you last night. I've been awfully worried about Esther lately. She means everything to me." He stopped and stared at a crack in the ceiling for a minute. I realized he was trying not to cry.

"Don't worry," I told him. "She'll be fine. I'll do her chores for her."

Uncle Dallas smiled. "You're so much like your father," he said. "You know he lived at Whistler's Hollow for a while when he was a boy. He stayed in your same room."

I wondered what my daddy did when he was here. Did he pick apples or rake leaves? Did he go to Paggett School? I bet a boy named Paul didn't bully him.

Uncle Dallas put his hand on my shoulder. "Lillie Mae, I have a big favor to ask."

I didn't think, I just jumped at the chance. "I'll do it," I said quickly.

"I need to get something into town, but I don't want to leave Esther right now," Uncle Dallas explained.

"I can take it," I assured him. I followed him into the kitchen, eager to help.

Uncle Dallas looked at me and raised a bushy white eyebrow. He rubbed his chin for a minute before shaking his head. "No, I suspect you'd better ask Paul Garrett. He'll take it for me. Do you know him?"

I nodded. I knew him all too well. I started to argue that I could do whatever Paul could do, but then I saw that Uncle Dallas held his violin case.

"Oh, no," I said, shaking my head. "You aren't going to sell your violin!" All my hopes of learning to play for Daddy disappeared. I figured Uncle Dallas needed the money badly or he wouldn't sell his beloved fiddle.

"Cash money is tight, but it hasn't come to that," Uncle Dallas said with a smile. Then, with his smile fading, he told me, "When you love someone, you'd do anything for them. I love Esther more than my life. The day may come when my violin stops playing, but not yet. Now, you'd better get to school before you're late. Don't forget to ask Paul to come over after school."

"Yes, sir," I said, hightailing it out the back door. Down the road I walked, thinking about what Uncle Dallas had said. Would anyone ever love me as much as that? Enough to do anything for me?

All day long I worried about talking to Paul. Talking to him during class would mean another spanking. Talking to him at recess meant wading through all his friends and avoiding a kick ball.

Before I knew it, the school day had slipped by and Paul had disappeared. Now I'd have to find him.

On the way home my feet slowed when I came to the Garrett mailbox. I dreaded seeing Paul again, figuring he'd tease me or worse. I wasn't wrong. Paul came out the door, took one look at me, and started teasing. "Hi, ghost girl."

If the gate hadn't been between us, I think I would have taken a swing at him. I took a deep breath and told him, "Uncle Dallas wanted me to get you."

I figured Paul would joke about Uncle Dallas being a ghost, but Paul wiped the smirk off his face and pushed the gate past me. "Why didn't you say so?" he yelled before jogging down the dirt road.

By the time I caught up with Paul, he stood in the kitchen with Uncle Dallas. I heard them talking, but when I came in the back door, they got quiet.

Uncle Dallas cleared his throat and told Paul, "You'd better get going. I appreciate your help."

"Any time," Paul said, shaking Uncle Dallas's hand. Paul grabbed the violin case off the kitchen table. Without looking at me, he pushed open the screen door and disappeared.

How could Uncle Dallas have let Paul take his violin? Jealousy surged inside me. I wanted to play. I needed to learn to play. Paul had a family and home. He didn't need Uncle Dallas and Aunt Esther. It looked to me like Paul had it all and I had nothing.

❧ 10 ❧
BLACK CAR

Paul took the violin case from Uncle Dallas every morning before breakfast and brought it back every evening. Paul would come in and we'd all eat supper together. Then we'd sit in the front bedroom and Uncle Dallas would play the violin for Aunt Esther. I would sit quietly, but Paul would laugh and talk with Aunt Esther and Uncle Dallas as if they were best friends. I wondered how friendly Aunt Esther and Uncle Dallas would be if they knew how Paul treated me.

When I listened to Uncle Dallas play the fiddle, troubles disappeared. The music was everything. It made me so happy that I forgot about Mama and Daddy for a while. Then when the music stopped, the world would come rushing back. Sometimes I just wanted to cry. I wanted to be able to make music like that so I could forget about Mama being gone. Whenever Uncle Dallas handed me his violin, I tried to play. I would stop only when my chin and arms ached. Thinking about Paul using the violin every day made me wonder how well he played. The idea made me try harder. I couldn't stand for him to play better than me. But never once did Uncle Dallas hand Paul the violin to play for Aunt Esther.

"I wish I was a better teacher," Uncle Dallas admitted to me one evening.

"You are a good teacher," I told him. "I've learned so much." Even I could tell my squeaking was improving.

Uncle Dallas grinned and raised one eyebrow. "I wasn't talking about your fiddling. I meant your whistling."

I had to laugh. My whistling had actually gotten worse, if that was possible. All I could get out was a little screech. It wasn't good for anything except to get Aunt Esther and Paul to laugh. I hated Paul even more when he laughed at me, but I loved hearing Aunt Esther laugh. We all tried to make her laugh whenever we could. She had gotten very pale. I could tell Uncle Dallas was really worried about her. He never missed a chance to do something for her.

Aunt Esther wasn't the kind to let a little sickness get her down. Unless she was sleeping, she kept busy. I never saw her just sit in bed idle. She spent most of her time piecing scraps together for a quilt. Her quilts weren't just plain squares like the ones Mama had, they were fancy ones with designs on them. "This here is a double wedding ring quilt," she told me one Saturday afternoon when I took her lunch, some soup that Mrs. Garrett had brought over. "My great-grandmother made it for my grandmother's wedding day," she said, smoothing her hand over the richly colored circles of the quilt on her bed.

"It's really pretty," I said, putting the soup bowl on the nightstand.

"The quilt on your bed is over a hundred years old," Aunt Esther told me. "It's like a history of my family."

I nodded. I was having enough trouble sleeping without having family history to cover me up at night.

"That's your family too," Aunt Esther explained. She held up the quilt piece she was working on. "This is for you."

"That's a double wedding ring," I said. "Isn't that for when you get married?"

Aunt Esther smiled. "Surely. One of these days some handsome man is going to snap you up. You are after all a right good-looking young lady."

She couldn't have surprised me more if she'd called me the queen of England. "Don't look so flustered," she said. "Dallas and I are in no hurry to get rid of you. We love having you here."

I wasn't planning on staying at Whistler's Hollow, so I changed the subject. "That's a very pretty pattern," I said, motioning to the quilt piece in her lap.

Aunt Esther smiled and touched my hand. "I know Dallas and I aren't your parents, but it would sure make us proud if you'd let us pretend that you're the daughter we've never had."

"Sure." I figured that was fine with me, at least until Daddy came home.

Aunt Esther bit off some thread. "Who knows, maybe you and Paul will even get married someday."

My mouth must have hung open. "Why do you let Paul come over here every night for supper?" I asked. Surely Aunt Esther could figure out that Paul was nothing but mean.

Aunt Esther put her sewing in her lap. Her voice was soft. "Paul's maw has never gotten over her husband being killed. She's not quite right—especially in the evenings. I'm hoping she'll snap out of it one day."

Every morning, I sat at the table while Paul took the violin case. I wouldn't look directly at him, but I watched him. Uncle Dallas would always chat with Paul, but I never spoke to him. One morning Paul came late, just as I was leaving for school.

"Isn't this nice?" Uncle Dallas smiled as he handed Paul the case. "My two favorite young'uns can walk together."

Paul and I looked at each other without a word, but left Whistler's Hollow side by side.

As we walked along, a big black car roared by. It looked like the car I'd seen at the train station when I'd first come to Henderson.

"That sure is a nice car," I said, trying to make

conversation. I figured talking was better than rock throwing.

"That's the revenuer," Paul explained. "He's out to get moonshiners and throw them in jail."

"Get who?" I asked.

"Moonshiners. You know, the folks who make illegal liquor. Didn't they have moonshiners where you come from?"

"Sure they did. But how do you know so much about moonshining?" I asked. "Does your daddy make it?"

"Naw." Paul shook his head. "My pa got killed in the war."

"I'm sorry," I said, feeling bad that I'd forgotten about Paul's daddy being dead. "My daddy was in the war too."

Paul just shrugged. "Ma and I make out okay," he said. "We get a government check every month that helps out a lot."

I felt a little sorry for Paul, not having a daddy and all. My daddy might be gone, but he hadn't been killed in the war. Someday he was coming back. I renewed my promise to myself to try harder to learn to play the violin. Besides, it was something to do while waiting for Daddy to come home.

I tried changing the subject. "I hope that revenuer catches those moonshiners. My mama said drinking ruined my best friend's father— turned him into a lousy drunk." Of course, having his son killed in the war was just as much at fault, but I didn't tell Paul that.

Paul looked at me without saying another word. He turned into Brumby's General Store and I walked on to school alone. I even tried whistling a bit. Maybe my luck had changed. Paul had talked to me and I had lunch with Alberta every day. Aunt Esther would get better, and life wouldn't be so bad. I had no idea how wrong I could be.

No one talked to me at school, except for Alberta at lunchtime. I had gotten used to it. Alberta had found me a set of old battered books, so I could follow the lessons. I looked forward to lunch with my only friend so much, but all that changed the day Paul walked to school with me.

Alberta had tears in her gray eyes when she whispered to me in the coat closet, "I can't eat with you."

My heart sank. Talking and singing with Alberta

in the middle of the day gave me a reason to come to school. What was wrong? She wasn't under the tree at lunch to ask. She was gone. She didn't come back the whole rest of the day.

Back at Whistler's Hollow, Uncle Dallas got grouchier and grouchier. I knew he'd been up most nights taking care of Aunt Esther. I'd been up nights too. I'd lie awake and listen to the noises. My feather pillow never seemed to drown out the sounds, no matter how hard I squeezed it to my ears. I'd heard Aunt Esther coughing and Uncle Dallas talking to her, but I'd listened to something else as well. Strange noises came from above me. Could it be a ghost in the attic like Paul had said? If there was a ghost, then why did Paul come over so many nights and eat with us? Why didn't Paul warn Uncle Dallas? And whose ghost could it be? Mama's? If it was Mama's, could I talk to her like she was still alive? Would she know me?

I wanted to see Mama again so badly. Sometimes I'd lie in bed, close my eyes, and pretend she was there. She'd rub my head and say it wasn't true. She wasn't really dead. It was all a big mistake. Then I'd open my eyes and look around at my little room at

Whistler's Hollow. I knew that Mama wasn't coming back and that any ghosts at Whistler's Hollow weren't going to be friendly to me.

❦ 11 ❧
EMPTY

Without Alberta to eat lunch with I figured I would just go back to Whistler's Hollow for lunch. After all, Paul had talked to me yesterday. He hadn't beat me up or thrown rocks at me. That was all over and done with. It should be safe to walk to lunch. Maybe Paul and I could even become friends.

The crispness in the air made me remember walking with Daddy to Old Man Henessy's farm. Walking in the fall was something Daddy and I used to love to do, when he had the time. The leaves on the trees blazed red and orange, just like he liked. Strolling with my daddy wasn't just a walk. It was an event. He could find multi-colored rocks that no one else would notice and make a game of cloud shapes in the sky.

I looked up at the clouds to find animal shapes in the sky, like Daddy could always find. I wondered if somewhere Daddy looked up at the same sky. "Looking for ghosts?" Paul's voice snapped from behind me.

"Hello, Paul," I said. "Would you like to walk home together?"

"Don't you get it?" he said. "I can't stand you. I won't be happy until you're gone."

"Why?" I asked, suddenly feeling chilled to the bone. Paul had been so nice to me the day before, but that was only because Uncle Dallas had asked him to walk with me. Nothing had changed.

Paul pushed me in the shoulder. "I hate your guts. Get away from here, ghost girl."

Tears brimmed my eyes, but that only made me madder. "I am not a ghost girl," I said. "Don't ever call me that again!"

"Ghost girl," Paul said. He put the violin case down and calmly folded his arms over his chest. "Ghost girl. Ghost girl. Ghost girl."

I wanted to run home with my hands over my ears. I should have run home. Instead, I pushed

Paul as hard as I could.

I caught him off-guard and he fell to the ground. He came back up and lunged at me. We both fell to the ground and started hitting. This was no scuffle. We were by ourselves in the middle of the road. Mr. Price wouldn't be here to break this fight up. I had the feeling Paul wouldn't quit until one of us couldn't move. I twisted to get away from him and my head hit the violin case. It fell open.

Paul stopped hitting. I sat up straight and stared. The violin case was empty. Totally empty— except for a horrible smell.

"What did you do with Uncle Dallas's violin?" I asked.

"I didn't have his violin," Paul said.

I wiped blood off my nose and shook my head. "But weren't you learning to play?"

"No," Paul said with a sneer. "You're the only one Dallas is teaching."

I stared at the empty case. Brown stains spotted the red flannel lining. That smell. It smelled like death—like the smell from the attic. It was like another smell too. It suddenly dawned on me. Melissa K. Reynolds's father had that odor about him when he'd drunk too much.

It took me another minute to figure it out. Then I couldn't believe I had been so stupid. The noises in the night, taking the case into town every day, the revenuer, and the horrible smell—it all fit together.

"Moonshine!" I yelled. "Uncle Dallas is making moonshine!"

Paul leaped toward me and covered my mouth with his hand. "Be quiet, you idiot," he warned. I nodded my head and he slowly took his hand away.

"What are you going to do?" he said.

I shook my head and stared at the case. "I can't believe Uncle Dallas would do something so horrible," I whispered.

Paul stiffened his back. "Dallas makes sure everything is clean. He's not like some who poison people."

"The violin case is so small," I said. "How can he fit bottles in there?"

Paul closed the lid on the violin case and snapped it shut. "We use small, flat bottles so the revenuer won't suspect. We sell a little each day."

"But why does Uncle Dallas do it?" I asked, still not believing it could be true. I'd heard some people who'd had bad homemade liquor went blind or died.

"It's not something he's proud of," Paul said, looking down at the case. "He can't get much money for his corn or tobacco. He needs the money for the doctor and medicine. Miss Esther has been sick a lot."

It all made sense. I knew Uncle Dallas would do anything for Aunt Esther, even if it meant breaking the law. It didn't seem right that he should have to break the law just to buy medicine. That's the way it was though.

"Are you going to tell?" Paul asked.

I didn't know what Paul was talking about. "I don't know what to do," I said. I hopped up from the road and ran home. I had told Paul the truth. I really didn't know what to do.

❧ 12 ❧
THE BOX

I didn't know what Aunt Esther had said in that letter she had written so long ago to Aunt Helen, but it must have been a doozy. By the time I got home, wiped the dust off my dress, washed my face, and said hello to Aunt Esther, a postman had his truck stopped at the metal mailbox. Through the lace curtains in Aunt Esther's bedroom I saw him lift a box out of his truck.

"What's Charlie up to now?" Aunt Esther said, hearing the truck stop out front. She couldn't see him from her bed, but she recognized the sound. We didn't get all that many trucks out our way.

"It looks like he has a package," I told Aunt Esther.

"Run down and see what it is," she said.

I dashed down the steps and out the front door. "Hello there," Charlie said as he lugged a good-sized box up the sidewalk. "You must be Lillie Mae."

"Yes, sir," I said. "It's nice to meet you. Aunt Esther wondered what's in the package."

"I reckon you'll just have to open it and tell her," Charlie said around a chaw of tobacco. "This here package is for you."

"Me?" I'd never even gotten a letter in the mail, let alone a big box.

"Give my best to Esther and Dallas," Charlie said, tipping his hat to me after he'd put the box inside the door.

I looked at the neatly printed letters on the box.

LILLIE MAE WORTH
WHISTLER'S HOLLOW
HENDERSON, KENTUCKY

Sure enough it was addressed to me, and the return address was from Aunt Helen in Louisville.

THE BOX

"Who's it from?" Aunt Esther called from upstairs.

I took the steps two at a time. "It's a box for me from Aunt Helen."

"Well, it's about time she got around to sending you something. I gave her a piece of my mind. Imagine taking a mother's things from a child," Aunt Esther said. "Don't stand around yapping. Go open that box."

"Yes, ma'am," I said with a smile. I figured it must have nearly killed Aunt Helen to spend money on postage. Downstairs I worked the box open, wondering what in the world could be in there for me. There was no letter from Aunt Helen, but at the very top, wrapped in old newspaper, was my mama and daddy's picture, the very one that I'd longed for. I guess Aunt Helen must have cared for Mama at least a little or she would have sold the picture, frame and all. I ran up to Aunt Esther's room to show her and give her a hug. "Oh, thank you, Aunt Esther," I said with tears in my eyes.

Aunt Esther sniffed softly. "Well, it's only right that you should have some of your maw's things."

She took the photo from my hands and stared at my mama and daddy. "What a handsome couple," she said. "You surely do favor your mama, but you have your daddy's eyes. Those are beautiful eyes."

Aunt Esther handed the picture back and I stared at the black-and-white photo. I knew that Daddy's eyes were the same bright blue as mine, but the picture didn't show it. I had just about forgotten Daddy's eyes. I guessed anytime I wanted to remember, I could look in the mirror. I smiled at Aunt Esther and rushed downstairs to look through my treasure box.

I picked up each wrapped item carefully, fearful of breaking a memory. Aunt Helen had sent my baby picture. It seemed like yesterday it had been in our apartment, but in another way it seemed like years ago.

Underneath the baby picture was my Raggedy Ann. I held her tight, and then sat her in my lap while I went through the rest of the box.

Aunt Helen had also sent me Mama's worn-out purse. Mama had taken it with her whenever she went shopping. Out of curiosity I opened the clasp, but the purse was empty. The hankie Mama always carried was missing, along with the tattered coin purse that she'd counted pennies from. I felt around inside for any scrap of paper Mama might have written a grocery list on, but there was nothing there. Only a faint smell of Mama's dusting powder remained.

I swallowed and kept the purse in my lap with my doll. It felt good to touch something of Mama's, even if it was empty. I checked to see what else was in the box. All that was left were two big bundles of old letters. It surprised me that Aunt Helen had bothered to keep them. I pulled out one. It was one of Daddy's war letters—addressed to Mama. How Mama and I had looked forward to those letters. There had been so many at first, then precious few near the end of the war. I opened the letter up and wondered if Daddy would mind if I read it. Maybe he'd said things in there that he hadn't wanted me to see, but then I remembered that Mama had read every letter out loud to me, at least every letter that I knew about. I'd probably already heard this one anyway. I decided to read.

Dear Patty,

I mark the days off on a little calendar I keep in my pocket. Every day that I cross away means a day closer to the time I get to see you and Lillie Mae again. I miss you both so much. It's hard being alone.

That's as far as I got. I held the letter to my chest and it burned a hole in my heart. Daddy would never get to see Mama again. I squeezed my eyes tight, shutting out the awful little service Aunt Helen had put on for Mama. I wanted to forget the minister from Aunt Helen's church with the yellow teeth and the way he'd winced when he said Mama's name.

I wished I could roll back time and tell Mama not to work at the factory. But she'd had to work to buy food for us to eat. She had to keep us alive, because we both prayed that somehow Daddy would come home. But it wouldn't matter now, because she'd never see him again.

I heard a creak on the stairs and saw Aunt Esther. She was so soft looking in her faded nightgown that a puff of wind would have blown her away, but she came to me and held me in strong arms. That was when I couldn't hold it in anymore. The sobs came in jerks, and Aunt Esther stroked my hair. "It's all right to cry," she told me. "We all need to cry."

I did cry. Cried for Daddy because he'd never see Mama again. He didn't even get to see her laid out in Aunt Helen's parlor. Didn't get to kiss her one last time. I cried because my daddy might be gone forever too. I cried for me, for Mama. I wanted my parents back.

Aunt Esther held me until I hiccuped from the sobs. "I'm so sorry," she said. "Maybe I shouldn't have sent for the things."

"Oh, no," I said. "Thank you so much for doing that."

I decided to read a letter a day from the box. Maybe by the time I was finished, my daddy would be home. There might even be a clue inside the letters telling why he wasn't home if I read them carefully enough. It was so nice to hear from him again. We hadn't gotten a new letter from him in so long. Even though these letters were old and I'd heard them before, it still felt good to hear Daddy's voice, so to speak. The day after getting the box I read:

Dear Patty,

Today I saw the Eiffel Tower in Paris. It almost reached to the heavens. Some of the guys went up inside, but I just stood and stared at the outside wishing you and Lillie Mae were here to see it with me. Even Helen would like to see this. Maybe she could find herself a husband here to put a smile on her face.

Your lonely husband,
Bob

I finished Daddy's letter and I knew that one letter a day was not enough. That night before going to bed I stared at the box of letters and memories that Uncle Dallas had put in my room. Just one more letter, I thought. It was twilight and a storm was brewing, but there was still enough light to see by. I got my glass bluebird from the windowsill. I put it on the bed beside me. It seemed like a way to have Mama and Daddy with me together. Their picture faced me on the night table.

I had to open a pack of mail that was bundled together with a string. I pulled out two letters that had never been opened. The first letter was a bill that I guessed had never been paid. In fact, the second one was too. I wondered if Aunt Helen had seen them. I felt bad that they hadn't been paid. Maybe companies made allowances for people dying and not being able to pay their bills.

It didn't seem fair that my two letters were bills, so I reached deep into the stack and pulled out another unopened envelope.

It was a telegram.

❧ 13 ❧
TELEGRAM

I must have sat for hours looking at the telegram envelope. It was yellow with "U.S. Telegram" written in black letters. It was just a little envelope, but it was just about the biggest thing that had ever happened to me.

I remembered when Melissa K. Reynolds's family had gotten their telegram. Her mother's screams brought everybody to their apartment door. She stood with the door open, staring at the same kind of envelope. She didn't open it, she just stared. Mama put her arm around Mrs. Reynolds and told Melissa to run down to the train station and get her papa, quick.

I ran with Melissa. We both knew something

bad was going on, but we didn't know what it was. I don't think we could have run the five blocks to get Mr. Reynolds if we'd known what was in the telegram.

Mr. Reynolds told Melissa he was too busy to leave, until Melissa told him about the telegram. He dropped the papers he'd been holding and ran. He ran so fast, we couldn't keep up with him. Mr. Reynolds wasn't exactly a little man; in fact, he was pretty heavy. I'd never seen him run. I'd never seen him hug Mrs. Reynolds either, but that was exactly what he was doing when Melissa and I got to her apartment. Mrs. Reynolds was crying like it was the end of the world.

"What's going on?" I asked Melissa.

She shrugged and looked at me with scared eyes. "I don't know."

Mrs. Reynolds thrust the telegram at Mama. "I can't do it. You read it." Mama looked at the other neighbors who were standing in the doorway. All of them looked down at their feet. Mama cleared her throat and opened the envelope.

Mama read, " 'Mr. and Mrs. Albert Reynolds, we regret to inform you that your son…' "

Mama didn't get to read any more because that's when Mrs. Reynolds fell on the floor and started screaming. "No, no! Not my baby!"

Mama left the telegram on a table and shut the door. We took Melissa up to our apartment and Mama explained to her that her brother had been killed in the war. Melissa sat at our kitchen table for a long time, not saying a word.

Mama gave her a piece of apple pie and some milk. I sat with her until pretty late, then Mama put us both to bed. Melissa stayed with us for a week, until her mama calmed down enough for Melissa to go home.

I told Melissa I was sorry about her brother, but she just nodded. She never talked to me about her brother after that. I never saw her cry, but she did. Her red eyes were proof.

Their life totally changed. Mrs. Reynolds wore black and I never saw her smile again. Mr. Reynolds took to drinking and hitting Melissa whenever he thought she'd done something wrong. I felt bad for Melissa. It wasn't her fault her brother had died.

The whole war was stupid anyway. Why did anyone have to die?

TELEGRAM

That night I didn't smell or hear anything that was going on in the attic. I just sat on my bed, holding the envelope. Deep into the night Uncle Dallas put his hand on my shoulder. "Lillie Mae, what's wrong?"

I didn't know if I'd be able to speak. My voice was hoarse, but I found the words. "It's a telegram."

Uncle Dallas left for a moment and came back with a coal oil lantern. I hadn't even noticed it was nearly pitch-black in my room. He set the lantern on the nightstand and touched my shoulder. "Do you want me to read it?" he asked.

I shook my head. What I really wanted to do was throw the envelope into the lantern flame and pretend I had never seen the telegram.

Uncle Dallas rubbed his eyes, cleared his throat, and sat down beside me. We sat side by side on my bed for a long time without talking. I felt so empty inside that I didn't have any words to use. Uncle Dallas stared up at the ceiling. Finally he looked at me and spoke, his voice cracking. "Your daddy was a good man."

I looked at the envelope in my hands. It was dated July 15, 1918—over two years ago. Mama hadn't even read it. She hadn't even told me about it. I wouldn't have even seen it if Aunt Esther hadn't written the letter to Aunt Helen. And Aunt Helen hadn't even bothered looking through the letters of her own dead sister. She hadn't cared enough. But Mama had cared. She had loved Daddy so much. The telegram had come and Mama hadn't even opened it. Why hadn't she read it? Maybe she couldn't. Maybe she had cared too much.

"Lillie Mae, I'm so sorry," Uncle Dallas said softly.

I nodded and looked down. For so long I had held onto the hope that Daddy would come fly me into the air with his strong arms like he had when I was a little girl. It couldn't be true that he was really gone. If I didn't read the telegram, maybe it wouldn't be true.

"No! No! No! It's a lie! It's a lie!" I screamed and ran from the room.

Aunt Esther met me in the dark hallway. She looked like a ghost, coming to me with arms outstretched. "Lillie Mae, are you all right?" she asked. I wanted to fall into her arms and let her hold me. I couldn't do it.

"No!" I screamed and rushed past her, the envelope still clutched in my hand. Down the stairs. Out the kitchen door. I had to get away from Whistler's Hollow. I had to get home. Home to Daddy. Home to Mama. If I could just get back home, everything would be all right. I would get there no matter what.

I ran down the road as lightning flashed above me. I didn't care about anything except getting home. I ran until my heart pounded in my ears. A huge black car, the revenuer's car, lurched toward me in a flash of lightning. I turned off the road and into the woods. I kept running. The woods grabbed at me.

I'd never explored these woods the way Melissa K. Reynolds and I had done the woods on Old Man Henessy's farm. Before I knew it, I was lost. Shadows were everywhere. I heard strange sounds. I didn't know if the revenuer had come after me or if it was wild animals ready to eat me up.

I huddled beside an old hickory nut tree as the rain blew against my face. I don't know how long I stayed there beside that tree, but my dress and hair were soaked through and through. The cold wind sent shivers through my body, but I didn't care. I just wanted my family. "Daddy! Mama!" I screamed. "Where are you? Why did you leave me?"

Only a flash of lightning answered me and I cried into the rough bark of the tree. The lightning came fast and often and lit up the sky. "Oh, Mama, please, I need you so much. Oh, Daddy..." I cried.

A gust of wind brought a black bird to my feet. It was my black bird—the same one from school. "What are you doing out here in the rain, you crazy bird? Don't you have any sense? Get home!" I yelled.

The bird looked at me and cawed. I thought about my own words and knew I was crazy to be out in the woods in a thunderstorm in the middle of the night, but I didn't have a home—not a real home with a mama and a daddy.

The bird cawed again. For some reason it made me feel calmer. I reached out toward the bird and said, "I guess it's just you and me." To my surprise, the bird didn't hop away. I touched it and felt a lump in my throat. "Mama," I whispered. For some reason I felt like Mama was trying to comfort me. I even thought the bird might have been my mama's spirit come to help me.

My mama had a beautiful soul though. If she was going to come back as a bird, it would be a beautiful bluebird, not a big black crow. Of course, maybe if you get to come back from the dead, you don't have a choice. Maybe you take whatever God gives you. Maybe it's not bluebirds sitting on your windowsill that brings good luck. Maybe black birds bring the luck.

The rain started up again, this time with a vengeance. The black bird looked at me, cawed, then fluttered off. "No, don't leave me," I moaned, but it was too late. The bird was gone. A loud crashing sound had scared it away. Something was coming.

❧ 14 ❧
WHISTLE

I wasn't about to let anything get me. I might not have a mama or a daddy, but I wasn't ready to die yet. I ran. Lightning flashed and rain poured, but it didn't stop me. I ran until my side ached so hard, I had to stop. I panted and listened. Whatever was out there was gone. At least, I hoped so.

What was I going to do? Would I ever find my way back to Whistler's Hollow? Would I die from the cold rain? Even if I found my way back, could I continue to live with Uncle Dallas, knowing what he did? I knew he wasn't a bad man. But surely breaking the law by making moonshine wasn't the only way to help Aunt Esther. Maybe I could help him. That is, if they still wanted me after the way I'd screamed and run off. None of that really mattered because I was completely lost.

The rain let up a bit, but the lightning and thunder continued. The lightning lit up the sky, but nothing looked familiar. I sprawled in the wet leaves and was about to give up hope when I heard a whistle. I scrambled to my knees and listened. Was it a bird?

No, it was a whistle—long and shrill. Uncle Dallas! He had come looking for me. I hugged myself. I wanted nothing more than to go back to Whistler's Hollow and get warm. I whistled back, or at least I tried to. My lips trembled from the cold, but I managed to get out a little squeal. Would Uncle Dallas hear me? I tried again. Squeak.

Unless Uncle Dallas had better hearing than me, he'd never hear my puny whistles. "It's me," I shouted. "Here."

The whistle came again. This time it was much closer. "Uncle Dallas!" I shouted, wiping the icy rain off my face.

"Uncle Dallas!" I shouted. "I'm here!"

The whistle sounded to my left. I turned to fall into Uncle Dallas's arms as a dark shadow emerged from behind a tree. "Oh, thank you for coming," I sobbed.

Lightning flashed and I screamed. The dark shadow wasn't Uncle Dallas.

"Paul!" I shouted. "What are you doing here?"

Paul put a blanket around my shoulders and pulled on my arm. His other hand held a rifle. "Come on," he said roughly. "I'm taking you out of here."

I pulled away. "I'm not going anywhere with you!" I screamed. Being lost and alone in the woods would be better than being killed by Paul.

Paul's hand gripped my arm so tightly, there was no way I could get loose, but that didn't stop me from trying. I scratched at his face and kicked his leg as hard as I could. He didn't let go, but he yelled. I knew he was hurting.

"Let me go!" I screamed.

Paul threw me over his shoulder as if I were a sack of potatoes and started off through the woods. I pounded on his back and screamed, "Let me go!"

We weren't going in the direction I'd come from. At least, the direction I thought I'd come from. Of course, hanging upside down over Paul's shoulder made it hard to tell where I was going.

Paul didn't stop until he came to a small shack. He opened the door and threw me on the floor. I saw stars when my head hit the ground, but Paul ignored me. He went over to the fireplace and soon a tiny blaze glowed.

"What are you going to do?" I asked, rubbing the back of my head.

With his back still to me he said, "I'm going to warm up, then take you back to Whistler's Hollow."

For a few minutes the only sound was the rain hitting the tin roof and the fire sizzling. "Why?" I asked suspiciously.

Paul turned around. He was a shadow with the firelight behind him. "Dallas asked me to find you," he said simply. "Dallas can always count on me."

"Why don't you leave me alone?" I yelled at him. "I don't need you. I don't need anybody!"

Paul stood by the fire without saying a word. I hugged the wet blanket around me and tried to get warm. I inched closer to the fire. My hands were so cold they hurt. The heat from the fire melted the ache away. "Why do you hate me so?" I finally asked.

Paul looked down at his feet. "I don't really hate you."

"You sure are good at pretending," I said.

Paul took off his hat and rain dripped off the brim onto the floor. "I just wanted you to leave Miss Esther and Dallas alone. I tried to scare you away with that ghost story. I was afraid you would hurt them."

I hung my head in shame. I had hurt them. Dancing with Aunt Esther had probably made her sicker.

Paul squatted down and looked at me. "I'm sorry," he said. "Miss Esther and Dallas mean a lot to me. After Daddy got killed, Mama had a hard time. Miss Esther cooked and cleaned for us for over a month. She wasn't sick then. Dallas never let us want for anything. Before you came, I had them all to myself."

I stared at Paul's blue eyes. He wasn't an evil monster. He actually cared about Aunt Esther and Uncle Dallas. "I was afraid you'd turn them in to the revenuer," he said.

"I wouldn't do that," I snapped at him.

"Well, I didn't know that," he snapped back. "I

thought if I was mean enough, you'd leave."

"I didn't have anywhere to go," I said miserably.

"I didn't know that either," Paul said.

Paul stared at me and I stared back. I felt a special kinship with him now that I knew how much he cared for Uncle Dallas and Aunt Esther. "We have to find another way to help them besides the moonshine," I told Paul. "That revenuer scares me."

Paul nodded. "He scares me too." Paul seemed so strong—after all he'd whipped me good. How could he be afraid?

I looked at the telegram wadded in my hand. "When your father was killed, did you get a telegram?" I asked him.

Paul looked at the envelope in my hands and his face softened. "Yes, we got a telegram."

I took a deep breath and slid my finger under the envelope flap. I pulled the yellow paper out and laid it before me on the wooden floor. I smoothed out the wrinkles and squinted in the firelight to read.

Patty,
  Not coming home. In love with French

woman. Lillie Mae better off without me.

Sorry, Bob

I scooted closer to the fire in disbelief. I read it again and again. I couldn't believe it. Daddy was not dead. I'm sure Mama had thought he was dead when she'd gotten the telegram, but he was alive. He was alive!

My heart soared and I jumped up off the floor. I felt like dancing. My daddy was alive! He could come home. He could take me away from Whistler's Hollow and Paul and the revenuer. Daddy could come.

I read the paper again and sank to the floor. My daddy could come get me, but now I knew he wouldn't. How could I be better off without him?

The more I stared at the soggy paper, the gladder I was that Mama hadn't opened the envelope. She didn't know the truth and maybe that was better. The truth was more horrible than death. Daddy didn't want Mama and he didn't want me. How could he just leave us?

I read the letter again with tears rolling down my cheeks. I should have been happy my daddy was alive, but I hated him. Right then I hated my own daddy. I wished he was dead. He didn't even know Mama was dead. He didn't want me. He didn't care. If he knew Mama was dead, would he come back for me? Somehow I didn't think he would. I didn't think I would ever see him again. He would never hear me play the violin.

The crumpled telegram fell out of my hand and onto the wooden floor. I stared at the fire, not even caring that Paul picked up the paper.

"I'm sorry," Paul said softly. "But now you do have somewhere to go. I have to take you back to Whistler's Hollow. Miss Esther and Dallas are worried sick about you."

"They are?" I asked, feeling guilty and wiping the tears from my cheeks.

Paul nodded and handed me the telegram. "It would kill Miss Esther if anything happened to you."

"Then I guess we'd better get going," I said softly, crumpling the telegram in my hand. I squeezed it tightly before tossing it into the fire.

Paul and I watched the paper burn before he banked the fire. We didn't say a word as he reached out his hand and pulled me up. He opened the door and we went out into the storm.

❧15❧
HOME

The icy rain came down in sheets. Paul held tight to my hand and pulled me along in the dark. The only light came from the occasional blast of lightning across the sky. Sometimes the thunder boomed so that I thought we were going to die, but Paul kept moving. He never faltered, although I slipped twice on the wet leaves.

When we finally got to Whistler's Hollow, I must have looked like a drowned polecat. What in the world would Aunt Esther and Uncle Dallas think about me running off like a crazy person? What had I been thinking? How could I run all the way to Louisville? There wasn't even anyone there for me anymore. Aunt Helen sure didn't want me. My own father didn't want me.

When Paul opened the kitchen door, the warmth of the house spilled out on us. Aunt Esther was downstairs in the kitchen with Uncle Dallas. She hugged me tight, not even minding my wet clothes. "We were so worried," she said. "What would we do if something happened to you?"

"I'm so sorry," I said, trying not to cry. "I've been so much trouble."

"It's all right, honey," she said softly. "Some things a body shouldn't have to bear, like losing both your parents, and you so young. It's just not right."

I listened to her like I was in a dream. Nothing was real, everything was in a fog. I wanted the fog to lift, but it didn't. I didn't tell her the truth about Daddy. Maybe someday I could.

After that night, Paul changed toward me. He walked me to school and talked to me like a friend. Alberta started eating lunch with me again and school wasn't so bad. But still I stayed in my fog. I just couldn't believe that Daddy had left Mama and me. With Mama dead I had no family at all.

One night all that changed, too. Paul came for

supper and afterward Uncle Dallas got out his fiddle. He put the fiddle to his chin, but stopped. "How's that whistling coming?" he asked me.

I shrugged, not really caring about anything —especially whistling. But I tried. I squeezed my lips together and out came the best whistle I had ever done. For a moment, my head cleared and I felt happy.

Aunt Esther clapped her hands. "Oh, honey, that's a right fine whistle you have there."

"This calls for a celebration," Uncle Dallas said. He looked at Aunt Esther, who seemed much better now. "No dancing for you, woman."

He let loose with a ripping version of "Old Dan Tucker." Paul surprised me by grabbing my hand and swinging me around the parlor. It was fun for a minute, but then the memory of Daddy whistling the tune got too much for me. The fog came smashing down around me.

I stopped dancing and started crying. Aunt Esther pulled me to her chest and stroked my hair. I knew I was too old for that sort of thing, but I didn't pull away. I stayed there, surrounded by Aunt Esther's arms. She smelled of medicine and sweet powder. I would have cried forever if she hadn't started singing to me. She sang "Amazing Grace" soft and low. She sang it very badly. God may have given Aunt Esther a kind personality, but God certainly did not give her a good singing voice. Her song broke through to me, though, and I looked up to see Uncle Dallas and Paul standing by us.

Uncle Dallas came and put his arms around both Aunt Esther and me. I knew that they cared for me. They were all I had in the world. They were my family. I vowed to do all I could to help them. I knew Paul felt the same way. I was home.